This igloo book belongs to:

....

igloobooks

Published in 2020
by Igloo Books Ltd
Cottage Farm
Sywell
NN6 0BJ
www.igloobooks.com

0320 003
4 6 8 10 12 11 9 7 5
ISBN 978-1-78670-319-4

Written by Stephanie Moss
Illustrated by Natalia Moore

Cover designed by Nicholas Gage
Designed by Matthew Ellero
Edited by Caroline Richards

Printed and manufactured in China

The Magic Handbag

igloobooks

Princess Annabelle flopped down on the royal throne and gave a **great big sigh.**

"I'm **bored**," she said to her fluffy kitten, Sparkle.

"I'm tired of pretending to rule my toy kingdom. What we need is a real **adventure**."

So, Annabelle decided to explore the palace in search of some fun.

Soon, Annabelle found herself at the top of a tall tower of the palace, in an old room she'd never been in before.

"Look, Sparkle," she said, "a **huge** dressing-up chest."
Coming from inside was a magical, glowing light.

"It's coming from this purse,"
said Annabelle, peering closer.
"I wonder what's inside it?"
She secretly hoped that this was the
adventure she had been looking for.

Very carefully, Annabelle opened up the sparkly purse.
As she looked inside, the light began to glow...

... brighter and **brighter.**

Rummaging around, Annabelle pulled out a pair of fancy sunglasses.

Annabelle put them on and turned to look in the mirror, but there was no reflection!

"I'm invisible," she whispered. "We're finally having an adventure after all."

So, Annabelle tiptoed unseen past the maid in the palace hallway.

She munched on one of Chef's best cupcakes in the kitchen.

The queen couldn't believe her eyes when the piano started playing itself.

And the royal gardener checked his specs when he saw a bouquet floating past.

Annabelle ran off into the gardens, giggling. "That was so much **fun**," she said, taking off the sunglasses. She looked down at her dirty clothes. "And look how **messy** I am!"

When she looked in the purse again, she found a pretty hairbrush.

"Perfect," she said, but as she combed her golden locks, her hair began to **grow!**

As it grew **longer** and **longer**, her dress transformed into a beautiful ballgown.

Before they knew it, Annabelle and Sparkle found themselves
at a grand royal ball. "Everyone looks so elegant," said Annabelle,
looking around the beautiful ballroom.

Annabelle loved watching the princes and princesses whirl around the dance floor.

Sparkle even joined in the fun!

Suddenly, the clock began to chime.
BONG! BONG!

In the blink of an eye, Annabelle was back in the palace gardens. "Let's see what else is inside the purse," she said.

Annabelle tipped everything out of the bag. "A ring!" she cried, slipping it onto her finger.

As the ring glowed, Annabelle began to float above the ground.

"I can fly!" she cried. ZOOM!
She flew up into the air and whizzed
to the top of the palace.

She WHOOSHED around
the turrets, doing loop-the-loops.
"WHEEEE!" she cried, then she
landed at the palace stables.

"Hello, Blossom," said
Annabelle to her pretty pony.
"I wonder if there's anything in my
purse for you to eat?" She pulled
out a little bag full of magical dust.

Magic
Dust

Annabelle sprinkled the sparkly dust all over Blossom.
NEIGH! went Blossom, as she began to **shine** and **glow**.
Before Annabelle's eyes, Blossom turned into a beautiful unicorn.

Then, she flew up into the sky, soaring over the kingdom
as Annabelle looked down below her in wonder.

Annabelle jumped on her back, as Blossom shook
her mane and spread her wings.

"That was the best adventure ever!" said Annabelle, as they landed back at the palace. "Surely there can't be any more surprises?" She looked in the purse once more and there, at the bottom, was a glittering, sparkly card.

"The Magical Wish Store," read Annabelle. "I can wish for anything I want!" she cried. Annabelle closed her eyes and thought really hard.

"I've had a great time with my magical purse," she said, "but what I'd really like now is a party!"

Annabelle made her wish and suddenly, she was in the grand banquet hall. There was a wonderful feast in front of her and everyone in the palace was having a fabulous time.

"It's been great fun having an adventure with my magical purse,"
said Annabelle. She munched on the yummy food and watched everyone
enjoying the party. "It's even more fun sharing it with all my friends."